UNICORN IN NEW YORK

LOUIE TAKES THE STAGE!

RACHEL HAMILTON

Illustrated by Oscar Armelles

OXFORD
UNIVERSITY PRESS

Unicorn in New York

STARRING

LOUIE THE UNICORN!

One Unicorn, One Big City, and One Dream to make it as a Star!

'terrifically funny and wonderfully absurd'
THIS BOOK IS FUNNY!

'A quirky and fun story'
THE BOOKBAG

'Louie the Unicorn is instantly loveable'
☆☆☆☆☆
AMAZON REVIEWER

'fun and fast-moving'
☆☆☆☆☆
AMAZON REVIEWER

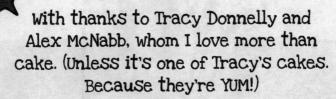

With thanks to Tracy Donnelly and
Alex McNabb, whom I love more than
cake. (Unless it's one of Tracy's cakes.
Because they're YUM!)

OXFORD
UNIVERSITY PRESS

Great Clarendon Street, Oxford OX2 6DP
Oxford University Press is a department of the University of Oxford.
It furthers the University's objective of excellence in research, scholarship,
and education by publishing worldwide. Oxford is a registered trade mark of
Oxford University Press in the UK and in certain other countries

Copyright © Rachel Hamilton 2016
Illustrations copyright © Oscar Armelles 2016

The moral rights of the author have been asserted
Database right Oxford University Press (maker)

First published 2016

British Library Cataloguing in Publication Data
Data available

ISBN: 978-0-19-274552-1

1 3 5 7 9 10 8 6 4 2

Printed in Great Britain
Paper used in the production of this book is a natural,
recyclable product made from wood grown in sustainable forests.
The manufacturing process conforms to the environmental
regulations of the country of origin.

Chapter One

Wakey, Wakey

Greetings, humans. It's me, Louie the Unicorn, back with a swish of the tail and a tilt of the horn to you all. I can't wait to entertain you with tales of my quest to become

New York's Number One Superstar Unicorn. But, first, I want to thank all of you who wrote in to say how much you enjoyed my first adventure and to ask for signed photos. It's fine that you only wanted photos of my friend, Arnie the Unicorn. Absolutely fine. I completely understand. He's a very dashing fellow.

Following popular demand—well, a letter from my mum—I have written another fun-filled tale of my awesome exploits at The New York School for Performing Arts. I hope you enjoy reading about them as much as I enjoyed having (most of) them.

The excitement began with a nasty noise, at very-early o'clock in the morning.

'Wakey, wakey,' screeched the dormitory tannoy. 'Get up. Get out of bed. Get down to the Main Hall. I want everyone there in ten minutes for an important announcement.'

'It's Madame Swirler,' Frank the Troll mumbled. He licked his hand and smoothed down his single strand of hair as he slowly blinked himself awake. 'She sounds grumpy.'

'How can you tell? She always sounds like that.' Danny the Faun reached for his glasses, missed, fell out of bed, and head butted the bedside table. 'Ouch!'

My other roomie, Miranda the Mermaid, continued snoring at the bottom of her tank. Frank and Danny bashed on the glass to wake her.

Ignoring the chaos, I leaped out of bed as fresh as a mountain stream. (A nice undiscovered one. Not one that Big Bad Mountain Trolls have used as a toilet. Obviously.)

'I knew it!' I clapped my hooves. 'I knew something exciting was going to happen today. That's why I slept in my clothes. Whoopee!'

Danny stopped banging on Miranda's tank to point out, 'You always sleep in your clothes because you think something exciting is about to happen!'

'Well, this just shows how right I am!' I said. 'Come on, everyone! I want to hear Madame Swirler's announcement.'

Chapter Two

The Big Announcement

I **pranced** along the corridor to the Main Hall, trying to convince the other students to form a conga behind me and enter the room as a beautiful rainbow of humans and mythical creatures.

Danny joined in. Frank tried, but found it hard to conga and pull Miranda's tank along at the same time. Other than that, the idea didn't catch on. It was clearly too early for congas. A pixie did grab Danny's waist, but I think that was mainly because he had sleepy dust in his eye and needed help with directions.

Refusing to let the lack of conga-support get me down, I danced into the hall and tried to find a place near the front for a good view. As the room filled up, I bounced up and down so I could see our Principal, Madame Swirler, make her appearance.

She shuffled on stage, moving with less grace than you'd expect from a fairy who was also a dance teacher. But, to be fair, she was very old.

'What bit her bottom?' Miranda whispered.

'Maybe she's moon walking?' I whispered back.

Miranda screwed up her face. 'Looks more like she stepped in troll dung.'

'Oi!' protested Frank.

'Shhh!' I said. 'She's about to make her thrilling announcement.'

Looking as thrilled as a spider at a spring cleaning party, Madame Swirler lifted the microphone.

'Good morning, students.' She cleared her throat, and started again. 'Actually, make that "average morning", students. As some of you already know, this year is our school's fiftieth anniversary. Personally, I don't understand people's obsession with birthdays and anniversaries, but the mayor has declared that there should be a celebration. So, in honour of fifty years of the New York School for Performing Arts, we will be holding a grand performance that, for one night only, will be staged on Broadway.'

Everybody cheered.

'The play we'll perform will be *The Handsome Prince and the Princess Pointlessly Stuck in the Tower*.'

There were a few cheers from the students who saw themselves as Handsome Princes, or Pointlessly-Stuck Princesses.

'Now,' Madame Swirler continued, 'Just because princes arc traditionally played by humans, it doesn't mean our favourite

unicorn wouldn't be great for the part.' She winked at Arnie, who was sitting in the front row, preening himself.

People say Madame Swirler is mean, but they couldn't be more wrong. Look how kind that wink was. She was obviously trying to make Arnie feel better, because everyone knows who her favourite unicorn is . . . ME!

Who does she pull scrunchy faces at? ME!

Who does she play hide and seek with? ME!

Have you ever seen her running and hiding from Arnie? No! I don't think so!

I felt myself glowing with excitement. A show on Broadway? My dream come true!

'I've never heard of this play,' Miranda

grumbled as Madame Swirler asked Arnie's Army to stop cheering so she could hear the sound of her own voice.

'It's a classic,' Danny explained. 'Once upon a time there was a beautiful princess, whose evil stepmother locked her in a tall, high tower.'

Miranda groaned. 'Isn't there always? I suppose the princess needs to be rescued by a handsome prince too, rather than just talking to her stepmother?'

'Shhh!' Danny hissed. 'You're spoiling the story. This is not a chatty stepmother. This is a nasty lady with a big key, who locks her stepdaughter up because she is too pretty to be seen. And no, the two of them can't talk about it, because the evil stepmother puts the princess to sleep for a hundred years.'

'Great, so the heroine sleeps through the action?' Miranda rolled her eyes.

Danny pretended not to notice and answered her question seriously. 'Yes. The evil stepmother also covers the tower in enchanted vines to stop anyone climbing to the rescue. And, just in case anyone masters the vines, she adds a scary giant guard.'

'That should cover it,' Miranda grunted. 'It'd certainly limit any chances for the princess to be a "shero".'

'You'd think so,' Danny agreed. 'But while she's sleeping her hair grows impossibly long. So, when the handsome prince has used his manly skills to climb the tower and defeat the giant, he can make a hair-ladder to get them both to safety.'

Miranda banged her head against her tank. 'Can't she even make her own hair-ladder?'

'Maybe her hands are numb after sleeping for a hundred years?' I said helpfully. 'She might have been leaning on them.'

Miranda shook her head at me. 'You're only making excuses because the role you're interested in is the role that gets to do everything.'

Not true. I was only making excuses because I wanted both Miranda and Danny to be happy. But she had a point about the role. It sounded great. I couldn't wait for the auditions.

Chapter Three

Top Tips

I was a bundle of nerves. I'd spent last term's auditions mysteriously locked in the school's boiler room, so I wasn't sure how to prepare this time round.

There was one obvious person to ask— my special friend, Arnie! So I approached him in drama class.

'Arnie, what tips would you give for these auditions?'

'My top tip—don't bother auditioning. It's my role.'

'Ha ha. Funny! You're such a jokester.' I patted Arnie's shoulder in appreciation.

He didn't laugh. 'You seriously expect me to help you?'

'Well, of course.' I smiled at him. 'We unicorns always help one another, don't we?'

'We do?' A strange glint appeared in Arnie's eye. 'Oh, yes, silly me. Of course we do. Well, friend Louie, let me give you some advice. Something I wouldn't share with anyone except a fellow unicorn.' He leaned forward to whisper in my ear. 'Stand out. Be different. Do the audition they won't expect. I hear Madame Swirler is a big fan of circus tricks.'

'Circus tricks?'

Arnie nodded. 'You know what they say . . . actions speak louder than words. Memorizing lines is so last season. Nowadays it's all about the circus tricks.'

I thanked Arnie for the excellent advice and ran straight to the dorm to find Danny, Miranda, and Frank.

'I need to learn circus tricks,' I announced.

'OK,' Danny nodded. 'First we have to tie you to a tree and stop you going down to the river until you do what we say.'

'Hunh?' I grunted in alarm.

'It's what they do with circus elephants. I saw a documentary.'

'I'm not a circus elephant,' I protested. 'I'm Louie the Unicorn and I do NOT need tying to a tree! I just want to learn how to perform thrilling feats of balance and agility with strength and grace. How hard can it be?'

As it turned out, it was very hard indeed. Miranda insisted the first stage of circus acrobatics was to master the forward roll. Have you ever tried to do a forward roll with a horn on your head? No? I didn't think so.

After Danny and Frank had unwrapped me from several duvets, moved the furniture to hide a large horn-shaped hole in the wall, and helped me out of a large pile of cushions and mattresses, where I was stuck with my legs flailing in the air, I decided to skip this far-too-tricky first stage, and move straight onto the ropes and the trapeze.

This involved a few technical arguments with Frank. Despite being a troll from Big Bad Mountain, Frank was also an amazing interpretive dancer (once you got over the sight of him in a leotard) and he insisted that, as a performer, the most important thing was making a beautiful line with your body. It was hard to make him understand that, as a dashing unicorn, the most important thing was ensuring your mane could swoosh gloriously as you hung upside down.

We agreed to disagree.

During mealtimes, I discovered a particular talent for spinning plates on my horn. The first few attempts were messy, but things

got better after the
dinner lady suggested
I use plates without food
on them. She also found me some plastic
ones after a couple of crockery-smashing
accidents.

I was similarly skilled at juggling. Some
people might take issue with this statement,
but, as I pointed out to my friends, it doesn't
matter if you drop a few things as
long as you keep at least one in the
air. Frank said this philosophy was
fine when juggling bean bags, but
not so good when juggling fire.

Since I'd decided learning with bean
bags was boring and gone straight for the
flaming torches, things got a bit warm for

a while. Eventually Miranda got fed up with having to use the water in her tank to put out tiny bonfires in the dorm room

and made me promise not to light my fire torches until I learnt how to throw them without dropping any. Spoilsport.

All in all, it was an eventful few days, during which I managed to strangle myself with a hoop, bruise my handsome bottom on the trapeze and, worst of all, get dust in my mane while practising cartwheels.

As I gazed at the dust flecks in horror, Frank patted me sympathetically and asked, 'Wouldn't it be easier to simply learn the Prince's lines?'

'Don't be so last season, Frank.'

'What is that supposed to mean?'

'I'm not sure, but Arnie said it, so it must be wise.'

'Arnie?' Frank spluttered. 'Are you saying this whole circus thing was his idea?'

I nodded and Frank rolled his eyes.

'Is that part of your audition, Frank? That eye rolling thing?' I asked.

'What are you talking about? Vines don't have eyes.'

'Vines? What are you talking about? I thought you'd want to be the giant.'

'What made you think that?'

'Well you're big and . . . um . . . not at all scary,' I finished quickly, not only because it was true but also because I knew how much Frank hated the way everyone assumed all trolls were nasty and aggressive.

'I want to play the enchanted vines,' he insisted.

'And why shouldn't you?' Miranda gave him a supportive fist-bump. 'At least now I understand why you've been spending every spare minute practising your "Be a flower" interpretive dance routine.'

Frank nodded. 'It's the perfect role for me.'

I'd be lying if I said I understood Frank's choice, but he was my friend and if that was the role he wanted then that was the role he should get. 'Tell me how I can help you, Frank. Wouldn't it be exciting if the enchanted vines were throwing balls of fire?'

'No!' Frank, Miranda, and Danny shouted in unison.

Chapter Four

Fire!

The day of the auditions arrived. I was raring to go. I'd practised and practised until I could spin a plate on my horn and juggle three flaming torches—all while swinging on a trapeze.

Frank described this as 'a unique talent', Miranda said it was 'weird but original', and Danny said he had no idea what that had to do with the Prince role and insisted the whole thing was 'utterly pointless', which I translated as 'very creative'.

Madame Swirler's eyes widened as I walked on to the stage and started to set up my props. I could tell she was impressed. Either that or she had been hit on the back of the head with a particularly large and meaty fish.

Her fellow judge, Mister Curtains the drama teacher, cleared his throat and looked down at his notes. 'OK, Louie, it says here you're auditioning for the Handsome Prince. Which speech are you going to perform for us?'

'None of them,' I declared, looking at Arnie for approval.

Arnie gave me a little nod, with that same strange half-smile. He nudged a few people in 'Arnie's Army' T-shirts, obviously letting them know this was going to be a role-winning performance.

'None. Of. Them?' Madame Swirler's eyes popped out even further.

'Nope.' I picked up my plates and placed my fire torches on the table beside the trapeze. 'Words are so last season.'

'They are?'

'Oh yes,' I assured her. 'Actions speak louder than words.'

Madame Swirler raised her eyebrows. 'What planet are you living on?'

'Earth,' I replied helpfully. 'I didn't know there were other options. Shall I begin my audition now?'

'If you must,' Madame Swirler sighed.

I prepared to astonish and amaze the judges with my routine. The trapeze swinging and plate spinning was going magnificently until Mister Curtains suddenly raised his hand.

Did he want me to stop? Why? It must be because my plates weren't fancy enough. Fortunately, I'd spotted a gold-edged porcelain tea set on the sideboard beside the stage, waiting to be dusted for the anniversary celebration. I'd decided they wouldn't miss one piece and had grabbed a shiny plate. This seemed a good moment to introduce it into my act.

'What did that unicorn just put on his horn?' Madame Swirler screeched.

'Oh my curly whiskers.' Mister Curtains

covered his eyes with his hands. 'It's the Meissen porcelain!'

'No! Not the Meissen!'

'Yes! The Meissen!' Mister Curtains peered between his fingers with a shudder.

'What's the Meissen?' Danny asked.

'Only one of the world's most expensive porcelain tea sets,' Madame Swirler shrieked. 'Which is now spinning round

on that daft
creature's horn.
That plate alone is
worth thousands of dollars.'

'Thousands?' I paused mid-trapeze-swing and the plate wobbled precariously.

Moving with the speed and scowl of a man blasted from a cannon, Mister Curtains flew across the room, skidding across the stage until he was lying at my hooves, his arms outstretched.

'Hello, Mister Curtains,' I leaned back on the trapeze to pass him the plate. 'I'm guessing you want this.'

He nodded, cradling the plate in his arms.

'Sorry, Sir. I shouldn't have borrowed it, but it looked so shiny.' I tried a smile but didn't get one back. 'Why did you want to stop me earlier?' I asked to change the subject, as he carefully returned the plate to the sideboard.

Mister Curtains took a deep breath and returned to his judge's seat. 'I wanted to stop you so I could ask, at what point in the show you think this will be appropriate?'

'Hmmm.' This was probably something I should have considered. I glanced at my friends for help. My eyes met Frank's, and I found inspiration. 'Enchanted vines!'

'Pardon?' said Mister Curtains.

'I could spin plates and juggle fire to distract the enchanted vines,' I declared, the scene coming alive in my mind. I reached across to light my fire torches.

Madame Swirler rose to her feet. 'What are you doing now, you foolish unicorn?'

'Frank!' I said. 'Let's demonstrate!'

'Do we have to?' Frank asked in a wobbly voice.

I nodded.

Arnie's Army sniggered. Frank fanned his face and shuffled across to join me, rocking back and forth on his hairy heels.

'OK, Mister Curtains, Madame Swirler, I want you to imagine Frank is the enchanted vines.'

'You want us to what?' Arnie's Army laughed harder.

'Don't be rude,' I said, s u d d e n l y

cross. 'Frank would make an excellent enchanted vine. Tell them, Arnie.'

Arnie looked up in surprise. 'Er, yes. Be quiet

everyone and watch Louie and his pet troll.'
He ducked as Miranda flicked water at him.
'This should be, um, interesting.'

'Thank you, Arnie,' I said, keen to get
back to my audition before the fire torches
burnt my leg hairs.

I resumed my position on top of the
trapeze, plates spinning on my horn, fire
batons flying through the air. 'Be the vine,
Frank,' I commanded, 'Be the vine.'

Shooting me a long-suffering look, Frank
got to his feet and began his interpretive
dance. There were sniggers to start with,
but they soon stopped as people watched,
mesmerized.

Miranda cheered. 'Frank IS the vine. Frank
IS the vine.'

As more and more people joined the chant, I smiled at Frank, feeling hugely proud of him.

'Focus, Louie,' Danny yelled. 'Wobbly plates!'

Uh oh! I tried to straighten up to correct the angle of the plates, but in the process I threw one of the fire torches slightly too high.

There were gasps.

There were screams.

There was a feeling of an entire room of people teetering on the edge of a catastrophe, knowing what was about to happen but unable to move fast enough to do anything to stop it, as the fire torch hurtled towards disaster.

My heart beat faster with every juddering

moment as the torch tumbled through the air, inches from my grasp.

Frank roared as it landed on his arm.

'Frank!' Miranda shrieked in horror. 'Louie, you've set Frank on fire!'

Miranda was right.

Frank forgot all about being the vine and became the rampaging troll, roaring and smashing his body against the walls, the floor, the cupboards, anything that would extinguish the flames. Fortunately he put the blaze out quickly, and despite the smell of singed fur and his ferocious glare whenever he glanced in my direction, Frank seemed relatively unharmed.

But that wasn't the worst of it. As I leaned forwards to apologize to Frank, the plates tumbled from my horn, knocked my left hand, and sent the second torch hurtling towards the judge's table. Panicking, I grasped for the third torch and missed, batting it straight into the mass of screaming faces in the audience.

Chapter Five

Arnie's Audition

I closed my eyes and opened them again, hoping I'd discover this had all been a terrible dream.

It hadn't.

On the positive side, the first thing I saw was Arnie shooting a perfectly sculpted foreleg into the air to catch the third rogue fire torch.

Everyone cheered. I cried a little bit

with relief. Arnie nodded coolly, flexed his muscles, and thrust the torch into Miranda's tank, extinguishing the flame and provoking a coughing fit from Miranda.

What a hero!

But before we had time to fully enjoy Arnie's triumph, the judge's desk burst into flame as the second torch landed.

'Fire!' squeaked Mister Curtains. 'Fire!'

Danny leaped into action, grabbing the nearby fire bucket, pushing Miranda's tank towards the judge's table and scooping water out onto the desk. Miranda joined in enthusiastically, twirling her tail like a mer-sprinkler, ignoring Madame Swirler's squawks of protests and demands for an umbrella. Together, Miranda and Danny

extinguished the fire, leaving a charred table and two very, very, very, very, very, very, very soggy judges.

'LOOOOOOOUIE!' roared Madame Swirler, 'You . . . You . . . You . . .'

'You're fired!' yelled one of Arnie's Army before collapsing into fits of giggles.

'I wish,' Madame Swirler snarled.

'Let's all calm down,' said Mister Curtains, wringing water out of his now see-through shirt. 'I know we're damp . . .'

'. . . And angry,' said Madame Swirler.

'. . . And cold,' said a sopping wet pixie in the front row.

'. . . And a bit scared,' whispered a small girl sitting near the torched desk.

'Er, yes, and all those things.' Mister

Curtains sounded slightly less sure of himself now. 'But perhaps we could look on this as an exciting adventure? After all . . .' he added, brightening up a little, '. . . no one died.'

Madame Swirler made a strange noise at the back of her throat, like a blender trying to squish ice cubes. 'NO ONE DIED? NO ONE DIED? No thanks to this imbecile of a unicorn. Louie, have you completely lost your mind? Go to your dorm room, this instant, while we decide what to do with you. Whatever made you think it would be a good idea to throw fire at people?'

'It wasn't my idea,' I tried to explain. 'It was Arn—'

My explanation was drowned out when

Arnie stepped on to the stage behind me. Arnie's Army started chanting his name.

'Finally. A professional.' Madame Swirler thrust damp hair away from her face and shook out her wings, drenching a group of nearby students. 'Just go, Louie! Come on, Arnie. Show us what you've got.'

Feeling about as valued as a piranha in a bathtub, I slunk towards the door, cheering up slightly when I realized there was a bright side to all of this—things could only get better! I paused in the doorway to see what circus tricks Arnie had decided to perform.

I watched, open-mouthed, as he delivered a word-perfect rendition of the Handsome Prince's main speech, using no actions

48

except a couple of minimalist hand gestures.

Madame Swirler and Mister Curtains, both still dripping water, rose and gave him a standing, if squelchy, ovation.

Arnie bowed.

Shaking my head, I wandered back to the dorm, my mouth no longer turning upwards at the corners.

Chapter Six

Understudy

I lay on my bed and dreamed of a life where I hadn't set fire to everything. It was a nice dream, so I tried to hold on to it when my friends entered the room.

'Great news, Louie,' Miranda squealed as Danny pushed her closer to my bed.

'Really?' Maybe it really had been a dream. 'Does this great news involve me not having to leave school?'

'Absolutely! You're going nowhere. They need you as an understudy!'

'As a what? Is that my punishment? Being buried under someone's study?'

'Don't be a spikey-nosed donkey.' Danny poked me. 'Arnie aced his audition and got the part of the Handsome Prince on the spot. Mister Curtains pointed out that if they're making costumes to fit a unicorn, their only option is to make you the back-up prince, just in case anything happens to Arnie. Madame Swirler agreed through gritted teeth.'

'You mean she was smiling widely?'

'Er, sure, that's exactly what I mean.'

I felt as though the sun was coming out from behind a big black thunder cloud and the buttercups were dancing a can-can to greet it. I lifted my torches in celebration.

'NO JUGGLING!' Danny, Miranda, and the still-frazzled Frank bellowed.

'OK, OK.' I put down the torches. 'Then join me in a celebration dance.'

Danny twirled Miranda around the room, singing as he swung her tank back and forth. Frank hung back.

'What's wrong with Frank?' I whispered to Miranda.

'You mean on top of his best friend setting him on fire?'

I blushed and gave a quick nod.

'He lost out on the role of the enchanted vine to a wooden prop.'

'No!' I stopped dancing and gazed at

Frank with sympathy. 'I bet wooden props don't need understudies either. So you're not in the show, Frank?'

'I am. But that's the worst bit,' he grunted. 'They made me the scary giant . . . because I was so scary *while I was on fire*.' He glowered at me. 'But I can't be scary on demand. What if I let everyone down?'

'It won't happen,' I reassured him. 'Worst case scenario, I can throw fire at you again.'

Frank punched me.

Nursing a dead leg and a wounded expression, I made my way to Madame Swirler's office to thank her for the understudy opportunity.

The minute I pushed open her door I could see something was wrong. She didn't even try to play hide and seek. She just sat there, staring at me blankly. I don't think she heard my thanks, or my apology for her earlier drenching. She didn't even call me 'foolish unicorn'.

This was unprecedented. Had she lost her voice?

I looked around her room for an explanation. The photos on the walls caught my eye. One in particular. It showed Madame Swirler standing outside school on the day it first opened—fifty years ago—and she looked exactly the same! Unbelievable! Madame Swirler hadn't changed at all in five decades. She had been old FOREVER. Our Principal must be about a million years old. I peered at the picture of her shaking

hands with the Mayor. There was a rosette on her jacket. I looked closer and realized it was a badge saying 'Happy Birthday!'

Wow! Madame Swirler had the same birthday as the New York School for

Performing Arts.

I was about to tell her how wonderful I thought the birthday-sharing thing was when Madame Swirler spotted me looking at the pictures.

I'm not sure what provoked the attack, but with a 'HI-YAH!' battle cry, she launched herself across the room in a balletic dance move that ended with a high-kick to the exact spot on my leg Frank had punched earlier.

Eyes watering, I stumbled out into the corridor, wondering why all my favourite people kept walloping me.

Chapter Seven

Method Acting

Preparations for the play were under way. Mister Curtains suggested I shadow Arnie to get a feel for the role of Handsome Prince. I agreed immediately. It was an honour to see a great unicorn at work.

Obviously I didn't want anything to happen to Arnie; but IF it did, I'd need to be ready to spring into action. So I shadowed Arnie in rehearsals. I shadowed Arnie in the lunch queue. I shadowed Arnie in his dorm room. I even shadowed Arnie in the bathroom until Frank pointed out that lurking by toilet cubicles wasn't what dashing unicorns should be doing with their free time.

So, except for the toilet, wherever Arnie went, I went.

Miranda told me Arnie would hate me popping up everywhere. But Miranda is not always right. As Arnie pointed out, everyone needs someone to polish their horn, vacuum their doormat, and remove the green Skittles from their sweetie bowl.

Miranda and Danny said Arnie was treating me like a 'dogsbody'. I'm fond of dogs and I'm sure Arnie is too, but I think the phrase they were looking for was BFF.

Frank seemed to have forgiven me for setting him on fire. At least he showed no signs of wanting to punch me again. But he was struggling with the whole scary giant thing—in rehearsals he was about as scary as a chocolate doughnut. Madame Swirler said if he didn't get his act together, she'd fire him from the show, which was unfair after all the hard work he'd put in. But what could we do?

The answer came to me when Arnie insisted I start referring to him as 'Your Majesty'. He was obviously getting into his role by becoming the character. Eureka! Method acting! This would be perfect for Frank.

So, the next day, I took him out on the mean streets of New York to begin his training. We started at the legendary Gleason's Gym.

'Right, Frank.' I poked the ropes of the boxing ring with my horn. 'Access your inner scary giant! Hit the punch bag.'

Frank took a half-hearted swing. The bag didn't move.

'Come on, Frank,' I encouraged him. 'You can do it! 'Imagine it's someone you hate.'

'I don't hate anyone.' Frank tapped the bag gently, barely causing a draught.

I was getting desperate. 'OK then, imagine it's in the way of a big bowl of green jelly!'

'JELLY!' Frank's eyes widened and drool slid from the corner of his mouth. With a hungry ROAR, he lifted his arm and whacked the bag so hard it exploded off its chain and shot across the gym. It bulleted through the ropes and into another boxing ring, where it knocked out a muscular young boxer training inside.

'Uh oh!' Frank lumbered towards the

ring. 'Hey,' he called, 'I'm sorry.'

I scurried after him, smiling nervously at the mob of angry boxer-types gathering around us

'You knocked out the champ!' A fighter who looked like he could be half-man, half-bear poked a finger at Frank.

'Yikes!' I tugged Frank's T-shirt. 'See how mad these guys look? That's the expression Madame Swirler wants from you. Check it out, memorize it and then RUN!'

But Frank insisted on apologizing personally to the guy he'd knocked out, and plodded on, moving steadily closer to the ring. As he approached, several of the boxers took a backwards step. I realized how intimidating Frank must appear at that moment—the troll who'd sent a punch bag rocketing across the room! But who knew how long that effect would last? Some of these fighters had very ripply muscles.

The trainer took the robe from the flattened boxer and held it out to Frank. 'The champ is down. Long live the new champ.'

Frank gazed at him in astonishment.

'Join our club, big fella,' the manager said, still holding out the robe.

'Oh, no. I couldn't possibly,' Frank said. 'I didn't mean to hurt anyone. I come in peace.' He made a happy hippy sign with his fingers, which would have been more convincing if he hadn't been standing over the dazed-looking ex-champ.

The trainer snorted, waved for someone to

come and carry off the poor battered boxer, and continued thrusting the robe towards Frank. 'Whaddya say?'

'What do I say?' Frank folded his fingers away slowly and took a step back, murmuring, 'I say, it was lovely to meet you.' He grabbed my arm and lolloped towards the exit. 'And now I say goodbye.'

'Nice start, Champ.' I giggled as we breathed fresh air once more. 'You scared the scary guys.'

'I feel terrible about it. It was an accident.'

'Then you need to learn how to do it on purpose. Let's go to Central Park and practise.'

Chapter Eight

Watch Out, Pigeons

We walked through Central Park, following the winding trails, feeling like we were discovering its rocks and streams for the first time. This was the closest thing to Story Land you could find in New York, and as we wandered, Frank's breathing returned to normal and some of the creases disappeared from his forehead.

As he leaned down to smell the flowers, I

ran on ahead and hid behind a bush. When he approached, I leaped out and yelled, 'BOO!'

'Arggghhh!' Frank roared, jumping into the welcoming branches of a nearby red oak.

A few minutes later, he climbed back down again, looking sheepish. 'What was that for, Louie?'

'Just showing you how it's done!'

'You scared me!'

'That's the point, Frank. You're supposed to be a big fearsome giant.'

'But I'm not.'

'You just need the right motivation. Pretend I'm standing between you and your green jelly.'

'I'm not falling for that again,' Frank frowned.

'OK, forget the jelly. Imagine I'm standing in front of a doughnut.'

Frank shook his head.

What to do next? I'd run out of ideas.

Without warning, Frank suddenly sprang into action, roaring and shoving me back towards the trees.

I squealed in alarm, and curled into a small unicorn ball. I couldn't decide whether to ram Frank with my horn for terrifying me or to congratulate him on being a truly ferocious giant.

The fur on the back of Frank's neck was still raised as he growled at a jogger who'd picked up a stick. Frank must have thought

he planned to whack us with it.

'It's OK, Frank. I've seen this before. Humans like to throw sticks for dogs,' I explained. 'He's not going to hurt us. But good scaring, Frank. VERY good scaring.'

'I wanted to protect you,' Frank said.

'Awww.' My horn tingled. 'That's nice. My very own troll bodyguard. Do you see what this means, Frank? It doesn't matter if you can't be scary to scare your enemies. You can be scary to save your friends.'

Frank raised a pointy eyebrow. 'Guess so.'

'Let's start small. Pretend that pigeon up there is going to attack us with . . .'

I looked around for a lethal bird-weapon.

The pigeon watched me and relieved

himself on the branch.

'Pretend he's going to attack us with pigeon poo.'

'Pigeon poo?' Frank eyed the pigeon with mild dislike.

'Come on Frank. You can do it!'

Rubbing his hands together and slapping the tops of his arms, Frank psyched himself up. Twenty minutes later he managed to successfully scare the pigeon off its branch.

Then he chased after it to apologize.

When Frank was satisfied the pigeon had forgiven him, we went to the Sunshine Café to celebrate the discovery of his inner giant.

I bought Frank one of his favourite red velvet cupcakes.

'Yum! Thank you, Louie!' Frank rocked back on his chair and beamed, his mouth full of cream cheese frosting. 'I feel good! Finally! I think I can do this giant thing if I imagine I'm protecting the princess rather than scaring the prince. And I'll be performing at the school's anniversary celebrations. It's like all my birthdays rolled into one.'

'Anniversaries . . . Birthdays . . . That's it!' I

remembered the picture in Madame Swirler's office. 'Frank, it's Madame Swirler's birthday on the same day as the school anniversary. Maybe that's why she's so grumpy. She must be thinking that because she's really, really old no one will be interested in her birthday. We have to prove her wrong and celebrate her old age in the most exciting way possible. Hurrah for old fairies!'

I spent the next couple of days spreading the word about the birthday to end all birthdays. (When I say that, I obviously don't mean literally—I wanted Madame Swirler to live for another zillion years—I just wanted her to have a rocking party first.)

Most people were very supportive—Arnie, not so much.

'This is a stupid idea, Louie,' he said. 'You have lost focus. You forgot to fan me earlier, and where are my pomegranate seeds?'

'Terribly sorry, Arnie,' I said, jumping to attention.

As I tried to fetch the fan and the fruit, Miranda blocked my way.

'Excuse me,' I said, trying to edge past her. 'Understudy duties call.'

'No,' she said. 'They do not and I won't excuse you. Understudy does NOT mean slave, Louie. Stop running around after Arnie and do what makes you happy—even if it is organizing a celebration for someone who won't appreciate it. Arnie's just upset you're taking some of the limelight from him.'

I laughed. 'Don't be silly, Miranda. Arnie wouldn't be so selfish.'

'Oi! Louie! Fan! Fruit!' Arnie bellowed.

Miranda coughed.

'He's just playing,' I reassured her, as Arnie flapped at me with his foreleg and told me to chop-chop. 'I don't mind. Helping Arnie won't stop me organizing the birthday celebration of Madame Swirler's dreams. Nothing will.'

'As long as you remember that not all dreams are happy ones,' Miranda muttered ominously.

Chapter Nine

Flash Mob

'**She's here,**' Danny hissed from his spot beside the window. 'Assume your positions!'

I clambered on top of the table next to the front door. 'How does she look?'

'Hunched and grumpy. Same as usual.'

'Perfect.' I waved everyone into position behind the door. 'That means the only way her mood can go is UP. Ready, people?'

Everyone shuffled into place and I got the nod from Miranda that let me know the whole school was ready, although I couldn't see Arnie anywhere.

'FLASH MOB!' I bellowed.

Everyone streamed through the doors of the school, following the carefully choreographed dance moves, keeping time with the music that blared from the opened windows of the dance studio.

Traffic came to a halt as we cartwheeled on car bonnets, somersaulted around lampposts, and sang a hearty rendition of 'Happy Birthday (Later This Week)' to Madame Swirler.

The most impressive part was our banners. We had worked hard on them.

The main slogan was 'Congratulations on being really, really old!' and we'd added a few that read 'The oldest Principal in the whole world,' for variety.

Then it was time for my song, which I had written to the tune of 'Twinkle Twinkle Little Star':

'♫ Madame Swirler, you're so old,
But you're worth your weight in gold.
You may be almost a million,
But you are worth at least a billion
(dollars or doughnuts).

Please enjoy your birthday surprise,
Because you are so old and wise.
We hope that we'll know
everything too,
When we are as ancient as you ♪

`SURPRISE!`

As we yelled the final 'Surprise', I wheeled out a magnificent cake, every inch covered in candles.

'We didn't know your exact age,' I told her. 'So we crammed on as many candles as we could. It's a super big cake, so it should last for the whole of your birthday week.'

I beamed at Madame Swirler.

She was lost for words. No insults. No

wise cracks. I assumed she was speechless with delight, until she started shaking and her face turned bright red. I took two nervous steps backwards but was still within spitting distance when she started yelling.

'I hate parties. I hate surprises.

And I hate birthdays. I don't want to celebrate my birthday, so why on earth would I want to celebrate my birth week? Did it not cross your tiny mind that the reason I didn't tell anyone about my birthday is because I DIDN'T WANT ANYONE TO KNOW!' With a final snorty-growl of rage, she stormed off.

'That went well,' Danny mumbled.

At that point, Arnie finally appeared. 'You are soooo insensitive! Of course Madame Swirler doesn't want to be reminded of her age. She's like, so old, Louie. Why can't you get anything right?'

Everyone glared at me. So many different expressions of disapproval that vanished one by one, as people turned their backs and left me alone with my disaster. Alone, with the gargantuan cake, which still had every candle blazing. It took AGES to blow them all out.

I wheeled the humungous jam and cream treat back to the Sunshine Café, where my friend, and world's best cake-baker,

Victoria Sponge, asked me how everything had gone.

'Disaster!' I confessed. 'We worked so hard on the dance and the song. I don't know why she's so angry.'

'Can you sing your song to me, Louie?' Victoria Sponge asked.

'Of course.' I launched into song, only pausing for a moment when I heard her gasp.

When I finished she swallowed and then said, 'Louie, I might understand why your Principal didn't feel like celebrating. I'm not sure if you're aware of this, but ladies don't always like to be reminded how old they are.'

'That's what Arnie said! I wish I could be

more like Arnie.'

'Don't be silly. That's not what you should be thinking.'

'You're right.' I leaped up. 'I shouldn't be thinking, I should be doing. I will watch Arnie like a hawk—well, like a hawk with extra legs and a horn—until I've worked out how to be exactly like him.'

'That's even sillier,' Victoria Sponge said. 'You're perfect just as you are.'

I scoffed and bounded out of the café, ready to start my new life as an Arnie-alike.

Chapter Ten

Super-Shiny Shoes

The next day at rehearsals, Arnie ordered me to polish his tap shoes, saying, 'I want to see my face in every bit of these shoes when you're finished, Louie.'

This was my chance! To be more like Arnie I needed to trot that extra mile. I would not stop polishing until every inch shone.

By the time I returned those shoes, I'd polished them so hard even the soles gleamed, super-shiny.

The day of the dress rehearsal dawned. Arnie pulled on his shoes for the big dance number. As a SUPERSTAR, he naturally wanted to make the most of his part—not 'show off' like Miranda kept hissing. His solo dance went on FOREVER . . . (Sorry! I've spent too long with Miranda. I mean it went on for a brilliantly long time to ensure

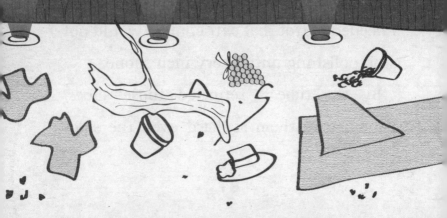

everyone could enjoy it.) When he finally finished the dance, Arnie began the run up to his dramatic Princely leap on to the enchanted vines.

To everyone's horror, his super-shiny-soled shoes skidded right across the stage, propelling him forward and whizzing him

through the enchanted vines with a cracking of wood and a crumpling of corrugated cardboard. Windmilling his forelegs frantically, Arnie flew off the edge of the stage and landed in a bruised and broken yet still-dashing heap on the chairs beneath.

I rushed to his aid, cradling his head in my lap, screaming for an ambulance.

Arnie was obviously delirious. All he could do was wail, 'Get off me, you moron.'

Chapter Eleven

Hospital Visit

I **hurried** to the hospital laden with grapes, flowers, and chocolates. It turned out Arnie had broken his leg. He was lying in bed with the cast hoisted up to keep it above his heart. The nurse explained she had done it to reduce the swelling and help it heal quicker. I gave her one of the flowers to show my gratitude.

When Arnie spotted me, he groaned—

obviously with pleasure—and pretended

he wanted me to go away.

I laughed at the joke, and told him I

wouldn't dream of leaving him in this condition. Besides, he had to smell the flowers. And eat the chocolates.

After giving him a big hug, I shoved a few grapes in his mouth, grinning fondly as he pretended to choke.

'Arnie, you're such a joker! What can I do to entertain you? Shall I bounce on your bed? That'll be fun!'

'Mhmmpf,' Arnie grunted, spitting out grapes and shaking his head violently.

I took this as an excited yes and started bouncing. Unfortunately, during one particularly big bounce I accidentally pressed a button that raised Arnie's leg even higher.

'Oops!'

I hit the button beside it in an attempt to cancel the movement. This was an error. That button sent Arnie's leg crashing down on the bed, making him cry out in pain. Flustered, I kept hitting the buttons trying to get Arnie's leg back in the right position.

Up. Down. Up. Down. Up. Down. Up . . .

'Arggghhh!' Arnie twisted and turned, trying to reach me, clearly keen to shake my hand and thank me for my efforts on his behalf.

In what I later heard the nurses describe as a 'super-unicorn act of strength', Arnie finally managed to pull himself loose from the leg-pulley and rose from his bed. Flipping himself upside down, he walked on his forelegs so his good back leg was free.

And, in a shock development, he used

that back leg to kick me out of the room.

'OK, OK. You're obviously feeling very poorly Arnie. I forgive you. I'll be back soon. Love you more than cake.'

'Grrr,' Arnie replied, toppling into the arms of a not-quite-strong-enough, red-faced nurse. Together they collapsed over on to the floor in a grumpy heap.

Chapter Twelve

Swoon

AS I walked back into the School for Performing Arts, Mister Curtains pulled me into Madame Swirler's office. 'I've just heard from the hospital. It looks like Arnie isn't going to be well enough to play the lead.'

'It was an accident,' I said miserably. 'I just wanted to—'

'So, you'll have to step in.'

'Whu—! Huh?' Everything went black. When the lights came back on, Mister Curtains explained I'd fainted.

'Why would I do that?' I asked dizzily.

'It happened when I told you you'd be playing the lead in the Broadway show.

Louie? Louie?'

Everything went black again.

When I came round, my cheek hurt and I was drenched in cold water. I looked up and saw Madame Swirler nursing the fingers of her right hand and waving an empty bucket in her left.

'Get up, idiot unicorn!' she yelled.

I grinned at her foolishly, delighted by the words. 'You're feeling better!'

She raised an eyebrow. 'Hmmm. You're right. Punching you has improved my mood. You might want to disappear before I do it again! Now go and practise! There are only twenty-four hours until the show!'

'Fear not, fair Principal. I know this part like I know the back of my hand.'

'You don't have hands.'

'That is an excellent point. What I should have said was I know this part like I'd know the back of my hand if I had a hand.'

'Encouraging,' Madame Swirler said, drily.

But I did. After weeks of shadowing Arnie, I knew the role of Handsome Prince inside out, and back to front, and dangling upside down. Which was lucky because I had a special project to work on at the same time as rehearsing.

By the following morning, I was drop-down-on-my-belly exhausted, but so excited it would take at least ten exclamation marks to represent my buzzycrazyhappyjoyfulness!!!!!!!!!!

The only blip on my horizon of joy was Frank's instruction to 'break a leg!'

'Frank! Please! Our dear friend Arnie actually did break his leg in pursuit of this role and it's no laughing matter.'

'It's just a saying, Louie,' Frank protested, 'Humans use it. It means good luck.'

'Don't be silly, Frank. There is nothing lucky about poor Arnie's condition. You're lucky I'm too busy to be cross with you. I have so many things to do before I go on stage.'

I didn't want to say anything about my project—even to Frank—the memory of the humiliation of the flash mob disaster was too fresh in my mind. But I was quietly confident in my new plan. I set up the

PowerPoint projector and tied a ribbon around the big book I'd put together, adding a little note wishing Madame Swirler a HAPPY BIRTHDAY. Then I left it on her chair.

Chapter Thirteen

'Action!'

Wow! The Broadway theatre was so much bigger and grander than the school auditorium. More than a thousand people were in the audience. They took their seats and 'ooohed' and 'ahhhhed' in appreciation as the play began. I watched the first half from the wings because the Handsome Prince didn't enter until the second half.

The story of the play had changed slightly since Danny shared it with us that first afternoon—mainly because Miranda had been extremely shouty with her views on pointless princesses.

The princess now had an intellectual debate with her stepmother about the rights and wrongs of tower-imprisonment (although she still got locked up afterwards). The princess also got to make her own ladder from her incredibly long hair.

Which meant it was time for ME!

I was on fire! Not with proper flames or anything—it was against the theatre rules to bring my fire torches—I mean I stormed the early scenes of my first Broadway appearance. I was imagining my Oscar acceptance speech, when suddenly things started to go wrong.

Frank had frozen.

This was supposed to be our big scene: the part where the Handsome Unicorn Prince (ME!) climbs the bit-too-wobbly-after-being-knocked-down-by-Arnie-and-then-nailed-back-together-again enchanted vines to challenge the scary giant (Frank) and win the heart of the Princess.

I'd climbed half-way up the vines and was dangling, waiting for Frank to go full-on angry giant, but Frank wasn't moving.

He was frozen in place, muttering, 'Can't do it. Can't. I'm a nice troll. Not an angry monster. I'm not like the others. I'm a nice troll.'

I clung to the wobbly vine and tried not to panic. Think, Louie, think! How could I follow the script of the battle scene if Frank refused to speak? There was no choice—I had to improvise. Arnie had been right all along. Circus skills would save the day.

I swung around the enchanted vines— mentally congratulating Mister Curtains for choosing the wooden structure instead of giving the role to Frank, who'd have been much harder to swing around, and climbed to the top of the tower. Seeing Frank was in trouble, Miranda and Danny encouraged the crowd to roar their support.

A few members of Arnie's Army threw rotten tomatoes at me. Perfect! I caught five of them and began my amazing juggling trick.

The crowd yelled out for more.

While they were shouting, I stood on tippy-hooves and hissed, 'You can do it, Frank. Find your inner giant and hear him roar!'

Frank stared at me blankly.

'ROAR, FRANK!' I pleaded, wobbling as another tomato walloped me in the head.

Frank blinked. 'Look out, Louie! Arnie's Army are attacking you.'

'No, no,' I reassured him as another tomato smacked into my face. 'They're just trying to help my juggling trick.'

'CYCLOPS POO! Those mongrels are attacking you—and it's my fault! HOW DARE THEY?' Frank raised his voice and turned to the crowd, singling out Arnie's Army in the second row.

'ROOOAAAAAAARRRRRR!' he bellowed, giving the best scary giant performance of his life.

He was so convincing half of Arnie's Army fled for the door.

Even I got the shivers, but I reminded myself I was a great actor and threw myself into the battle scene with vigour and a swoosh-ing-mane.

The crowd sprang to their feet at the end, throwing flowers on stage for Frank and me. I guess they'd run out of tomatoes.

I tried to juggle the flowers but they were a bit floppy. I didn't care. This was the best evening of my life. The world didn't get better than this.

Chapter Fourteen

Happy Birthday

I **was** so busy exploding with smileyness I almost forgot my special project. But I could never forget my favourite teacher.

As the clapping and cheering for the performance died down I moved to the front of the stage.

'Ladies and gentlemen,' I began, hoping this description covered everyone, both human and mythical. 'There is one person in particular we have to thank for this wonderful evening. One person who represents everything magical and magnificent about the New York School for Performing Arts . . .' I pressed the button for the projector, and tried not to squeal as the screen dropped from the ceiling, missing me by inches.

'This is my tribute to MADAME SWIRLER!' I announced with a flourish, before adding quickly, 'Who is not at all old!'

Miranda made throat-slicing hand gestures, so I moved on quickly to show the amazing images I'd found when I went through the archives of the school's

history the previous
night.

All of Madame Swirler's
achievements had been
captured in beautiful old

112

photos—images of her starring in ballets, plays, jazz numbers, and even dressed as a clown. Admittedly, quite a grumpy clown, but a clown nonetheless.

There were newspaper clippings too, with rave reviews of all her performances. Every single one got a round of applause from the crowd.

I looked out into the audience and saw Madame Swirler rise to her feet. I gave her a wave. Other people turned to look and she opened her mouth to speak.

She called out the usual, 'Foolish unicorn!' But her bellow was softer than normal and she fanned her cheeks as she whirled towards the theatre exit, trilling, 'I can't believe it. Oh that foolish unicorn!'

The audience looked confused but I knew what this meant. Madame Swirler loved it! She loved it! I knew she would. Sure enough, as she reached the back of the theatre, the exit lights showed her hugging the book to her chest with a little smile on her face. A smile! That was something I'd never seen before—I hoped her cheeks wouldn't hurt later.

Back at school, on the way to dinner, I poked my head into Madame Swirler's office and caught her flicking through the book.

'I'm so happy you like it,' I said, dancing a jig in the doorway.

'It's all right,' she grunted. But her eyes twinkled. 'Tha— Than— Thank—' A huge coughing fit swallowed her words.

'You're welcome,' I said with a grin.

Sipping from a glass of water, she recovered her breath and said, quietly but clearly, 'You did good out there, kid.'

The world began to go black, and I had to remind myself to keep breathing. Praise from Madame Swirler. WOW!

I rushed over to give her a tight hug containing all the love and admiration I felt for my favourite teacher. After a minute she went silent and turned an odd shade of blue, so I let go. But not before giving her a huge, wet kiss on the cheek.

'I LOVE YOU, MADAME SWIRLER!'

Greetings, beloved parents,

Life in New York is as glorious as ever. Last week I starred in a Broadway show! I wish you'd been there to see it—you would have been so proud (and you might have brought cake with you). I spoke to the theatre owner about getting a star with my name on set into the pavement outside. He drew one on a piece of paper for me and said I could glue it to the floor wherever I go. What a marvellous idea. Particularly as I can just make a new one when it gets accidentally ripped up. Which happens more often than you'd think.

I've been thinking about becoming a troll psychologist. I helped my peace-loving friend, Frank the Troll, find his inner scary giant. This made me realize it might work the other way round and I could go up Big Bad Mountain and help the unicorn-munching trolls find their inner happy pixies. Frank said it was a brave idea but might not be a particularly long-lasting career.

I have made such lovely friends here— Frank the Troll, Miranda the Mermaid, Danny the Faun, and also our wonderful Principal, Madame Swirler. You'd love her— which would be nice because nobody else seems to. You would also love my BFF, Arnie. He's a truly dashing unicorn. We are such good friends that he has now issued a restraining order against me. I am not entirely sure what that means, but I'm assuming it's to restrain me from running too far away from him while he's on crutches and can't catch up. I can't wait until his cast is off and we can have fun together. What's better than one unicorn in New York? Two of course!

Love you more than cake,

Louie Xxxx

Oscar Armelles was born in Spain, and almost from day one, could be found with a pen and a paper in his hand, he loved to draw—anything and everything. As soon as he was old enough he collected all his crayons and moved to America where he studied Commercial Art.

After graduating he relocated to London and now he spends his time coming and going between London and Madrid.

He works mainly in digital format ... although he is quite handy with watercolours too.

Rachel Hamilton studied at both Oxford and Cambridge and has put her education to good use working in an ad agency, a secondary school, a building site, and a men's prison. Her interests are books, films, stand-up comedy, and cake, and she loves to make people laugh, especially when it's intentional rather than accidental.

Rachel is currently working on the *Unicorn in New York* series for OUP and divides her time between the UK and the UAE, where she enjoys making up funny stories for 7 to 13 year olds.

LOOK OUT FOR MORE ADVENTURES WITH LOUIE THE UNICORN.

HERE ARE SOME OTHER STORIES THAT WE THINK YOU'LL LOVE.

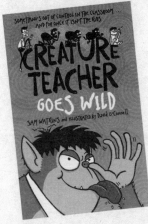